THERE'S A DINOSAUR ON MY TABLE

Hey, Johnny,

Look what I done did

Dear Dante,

You are my most

favorite Dante ever

There's a dinosaur on my table and a spider in my shoe!

03

Why is that box walking?
What's all this goo?

What's that noise?
What's all that
bumping?

6

Wow, that's a really big frog
And a lotta, lotta jumping.

Muddy foot prints coming in the
back door! I haven't even put the
mop away from cleaning that floor!

Oh, my days were once peaceful and as calm as can be. I could sit and read all day and quietly enjoy my tea.

No piles of toys or jars full of bugs, but also no sticky kisses or stinky boy hugs.

2

No bright eyes shining, no impish little grin, no morning cuddles to help the day begin.

No giggles or laughter ringing through the house. No, I remember back then it was always quiet as a mouse.

Thank You dear Lord for filling my home with laughter and surprise. This little lad is truly a blessing, though in disguise.

So, I think all the bugs, snakes
and yes, even those messes too,
Are worth it all because it means
I have you.

And you are my most absolute favorite YOU!

James 1:17

Every good gift and every perfect gift is from above,

And cometh down from the Father of lights...

Proverbs 17:6

Children's children are the crown of old men...

(and women)

Made in the USA
Monee, IL
11 July 2022

99415683R00017